VISION

JULIA GFRÖRER

FANTAGRAPHICS BOOKS

Look at you
oh...
Just look at you.
You're stunning.
Perfect.
Truly.

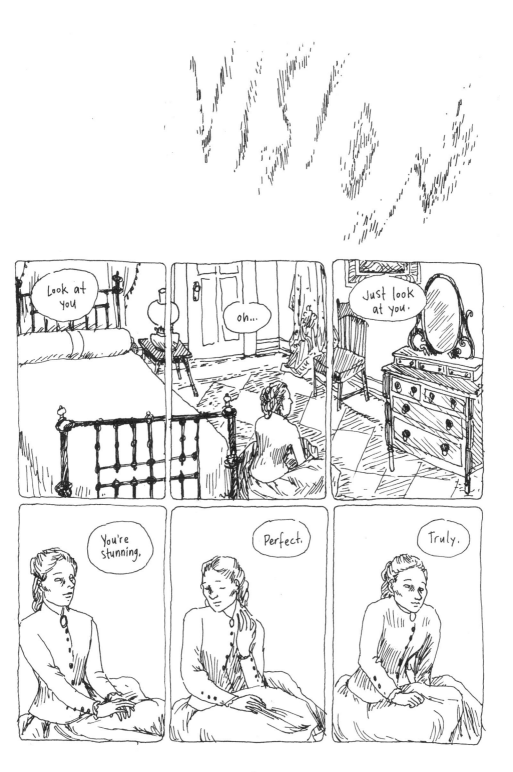

You're very kind to say so.
I'm not being kind.
I'm lucky you let me talk to you this way.
Do you want to take that off for me?
oh...
Little girl, you just cannot imagine
how utterly besotted I am with you.
Eleanor!

Eleanor!
Coming!
what's the matter?
You're wanted in the sick room
fine, fine
hm?
You look so queer
a little warm perhaps

Ready...
ahhh!
snkt
oh Eleanor thank God you came
oooh uhhhm
ohhhhh
ouuhhh
ohhhhhhh
ohhhh
ahhh
ooohh
There now, that's enough.
Now you must rest in bed until tomorrow
Eleanor, be a help and fetch her some hot beef tea
of course.

so good of you
this will be so nourishing for me
it tastes strange
Is it poisoned?
Did you poison it?
No!
of course not
it is shocking to me—
shocking how little regard anyone in this house seems to have for my fragile health

Please don't get up —
Doctor Bishop begged me to stay abed —
What's all the noise in here?
but I- it seems I —
Cora, sweetheart...
I must do everything myself
slam
Your sister hates me
fft
ffft

Is that a black handkerchief?
From when my father died.
What have you done?
Nothing.
See?
dried up already.
Good as new.

snif
ha ha ha
what?
That handkerchief suits you.
ha ha I know
black like my heart
and mine.
snrk
Enough of this.
Poor Eleanor.

No one to look after her.
No mother or father to worry.
No one to see how she suffers.
Her pretty eyes bright green with tears.
But I see. And I know.
Z z z z z
I know everything about you.

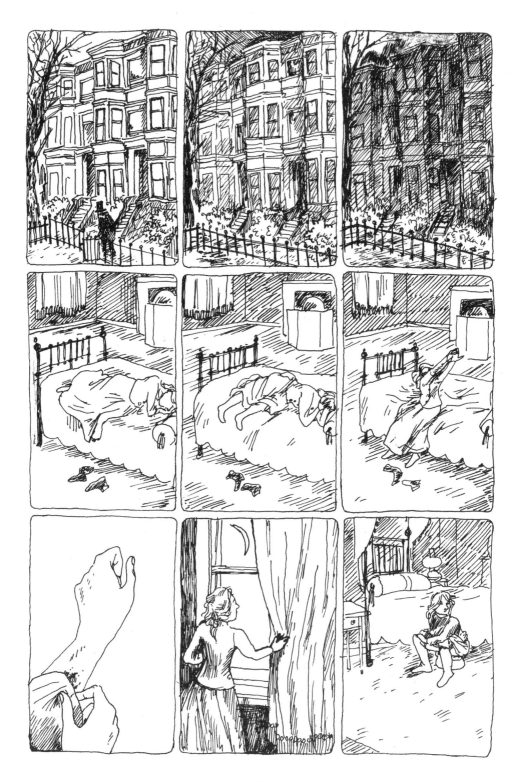

the hod's empty

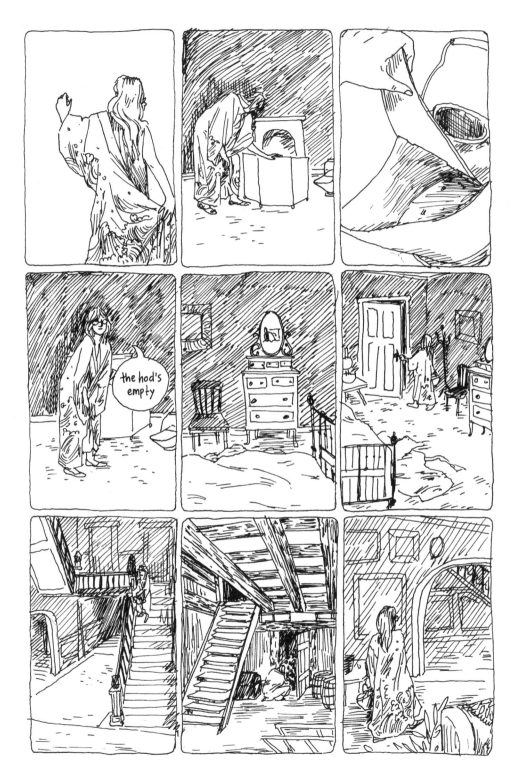

CLICK

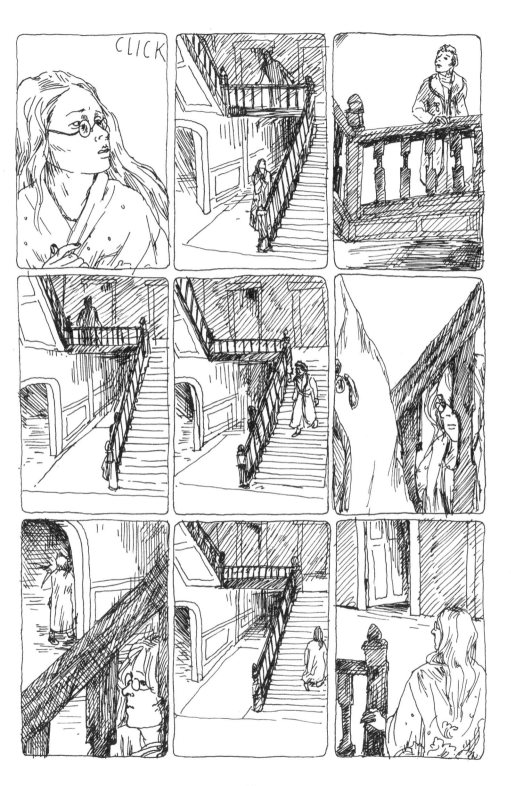

z z Z Z

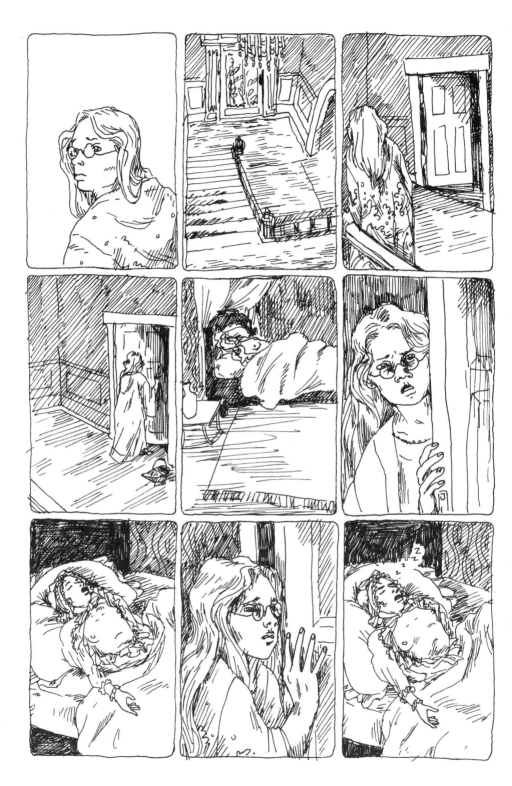

psst
Cora

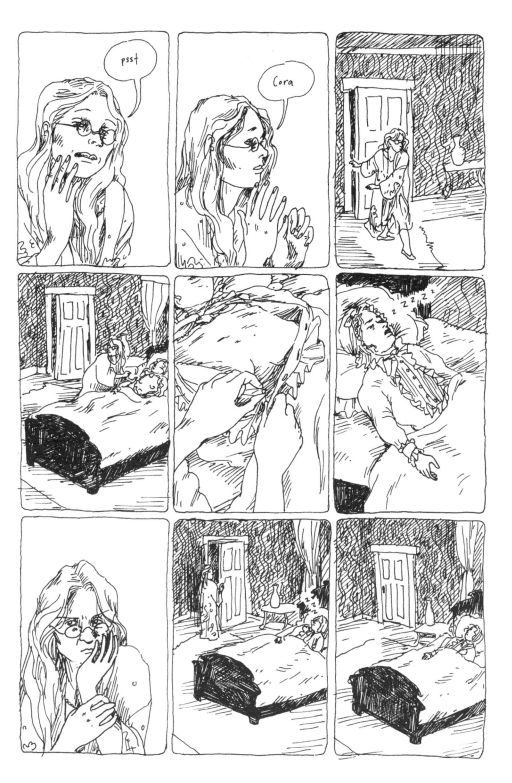

Where were you?
down in the cellar for coal.
I saw something strange, though—
Who was that man?
The one on the landing
My brother?
That's what I—
what did he want?
I'm not sure.
I don't think he saw me.
Come here.

Take off the robe and chemise.
Leave your glasses.
Thank you.
Now touch yourself.

more.
Let me see.
Does it feel nice?
uh huh.
You're very beautiful.
Now get something to put in there.

Get what?
The candle. The big one.
Good.
You were ravenous for it from the day you were born.
Before you even started bleeding.
Eyes always peeled for something to cram inside.
You were so innocent you thought it could get you into trouble.
Not that that stopped you.

You were longing
for men to touch you
before you even
learned to walk.
How do you know?
It's written all over you.
nnngh

Can I go to where you are?
It's not possible.
oh.
Believe me, Eleanor, I wish it were.
Are you upset?
z z z z

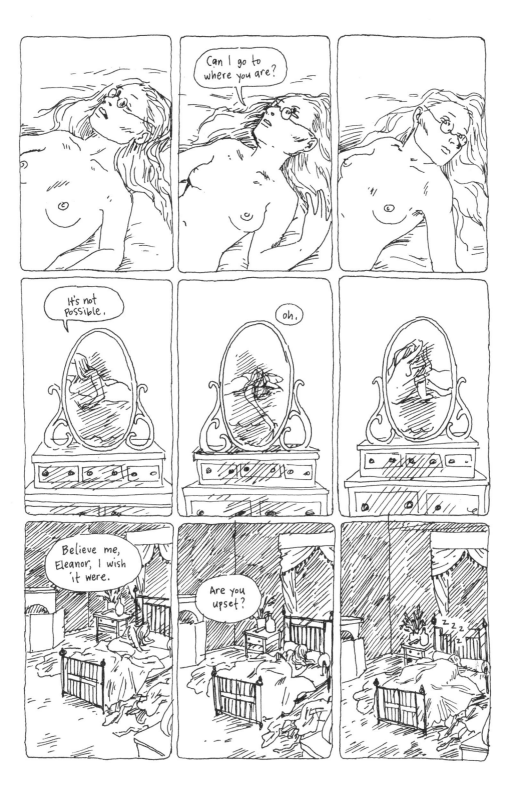

what were you doing last night?
wha?
I heard you, up at all hours. I didn't sleep a wink.
I got up to feed the fire
You can't lie to me!
I saw you creeping in my room!
No one in this house seems to understand I need my rest to get well!
What are you trying to do?
Uhh... Robert!?
Do you want to kill me?
Is that it?

I'm so weak
what's the matter? I'm coming in
Now Cora, what are you doing out of bed?
she says something kept her awake last night
Without sleep I can't heal
That's what the doctor said
There, there, Cora.
I'm sure Eleanor didn't mean to disturb you.

If Cora can't sleep we'll never have any peace in this house.
I know it.
She must have something for her nerves.
If only I had the time to call on Doctor Bishop today
She needs a maid of her own.
It's not as if you're busy.
Besides, she likes you.
If you were married, it'd be different.
How lucky Harry's death was for you, then.

Luckier still I didn't join up when he did.
Less so for me, it seems.
oh... Ella, forgive me.
He was like a brother to me. I miss him too.
I know you do.
It's all right.
Doctor Bishop will be in his offices until eleven, so don't dawdle.
uh...
You're a good sister.
something strong, tell him.

Don't dress so quick.
Don't dress at all.
I have to do an errand.
now?
yes, now

We'll talk tonight if you like.
I can't tonight.
Why?
Oh, my sweet girl.
I don't like to worry you
but to appear to you this way is difficult for me.
The pain is terrible. And every time it's worse.
Then let me come to you!
There's nothing for me here.
I want to see you.
I want to touch you.

Eleanor, sweetheart, you make me want to cry.
Don't ask me to condemn you.
I don't care—
Try to understand...
I love you!
I love you more than you know. But we won't discuss this again.
as you like.
I'm going.

Miss Lutz is here to see you, Doctor.
Ah! Show her in.
I thought you might have already gone
On Wednesdays I stay a little late.
Thank you, Mrs. Wakefield.
Please, sit.
I assume it's about Cora.
She says she isn't sleeping.
Oh?

but?
Well...
I've seen her at night,
No one could live on as little sleep as she claims to
...
She looks asleep to me,

She may be aware but unresponsive.
maybe
My brother hoped there might be some...
nerve tonic?
Something strong, he said.
she's disturbing him?
More the opposite, I suspect.
I see.
and yourself?
I sleep no more nor less than I would like to.

And how do you see?
worse again.
I wish you would consider—
it's not that I don't want to—
Modern cataract surgery is practically commonplace. The procedure takes less than half an hour.
The pain is no more than moderate.
yes, but the recovery...
You'd need to rest in bed for a few weeks, but the cataract would be permanently gone.
I just don't have the time.
I could speak to Robert.
I could insist.
Please don't. I do intend to have it done, just as soon as Cora is well.

Are you so devoted?
I don't think she would like the competition.
We'll consider the surgery deferred, then.
May I take a look?
Of course.
Tilt your head back please.
As I thought, the cataract has moved back into place.

Do you have time for me to couch it?
mm.
These drops will sting for a few seconds
hssssssss
hssssst

excellent
It has its full effect in a moment
Youre wide open. Perfect.
Ready?
Yes.
pop

deep breath now
forgive me
ahssssht
I'm not hurting you on purpose
rrrip
well
it is on purpose
But it's not the objective.
I see light!
Just keep still as I withdraw the probe... Beautiful.
Well done, Eleanor.

shfft
shfft
I've drawn the curtains.
Rest here in the dark awhile.
shfft
shfft

click
Belladonna drops, to relax and numb your eye as it heals.
And for Cora, Laudanum.
Give her thirty drops at bedtime. Don't let her do it herself.
Thank you, Doctor.

My love, though I may leave thee, be not grim
Nor fear those tides that carry us apart

Nor dread to navigate
with eyes grown dim
For ever thou art tethered to my heart
Raise high thy sails
and boldly shun the shore
though hideous maelstroms churn the pallid sea
and rav'ning waves assault thee aft and fore
plunge onward
for thy voyage ends with me.

Oh...
O dearest one
trust in thy fragile barque
to bear thee to my side
in endless dark.
Zz
zzz z
z z z

Z z z
Zzz z
click
oh god
OW!!
oh Beth oh no I didn't know you were standing there

ahhhh
that's—
snffff
That's all right
Miss, I...
oh God you're
bleeding
That's very
kind, Miss
why, this is a
mourning hanky—
I didn't realize
you were still—
you poor
thing
no, please
let me help
Eleanor...
Where's Beth?
Eleanor,
I need you

I'm here, Cora
I brought you some Laudanum from Dr. Bishop
You're to have it at bed time. Are you ready now?
If Beth's tired of reading to me, I may as well.
I asked her to take care of some things down-stairs
Let's give you your medicine and then I can read you to sleep.
How good of you. Yes.

it's um
30 drops he said
I'll just get you a glass
no need
all right
one... two...

twenty-eight...
twenty-nine...
...thirty.
smek smek
ughhhhh h
into bed
I need water
of course
ahhh
now where were you...
z z z

see?
Yes, I see it now
I see the wound, too, where he stabbed you.
How did it feel?
It hurt, of course.
No.
Give me more.

It hurt very much.
It hurt how? What was the pain like?
Round or sharp or long or short?
Tell me what it feels like in a body.
Help me to remember.
Please.
A sting, from the belladonna drops. Very hot and bright.
Once it fades, the pain of the operation itself is blunted.
Like a hard cramp, far away. A finger slammed in a door.

In fact, the pain would be easy enough to endure
but the probing instrument—
the violation—
touching as no man was meant to touch
There's no escape
A fingertip on the surface of the eye burns like a brand
The lid moves to protect it, but is firmly retracted
You can only be still and let him work
even if the unnaturalness of his touch drives you to the brink

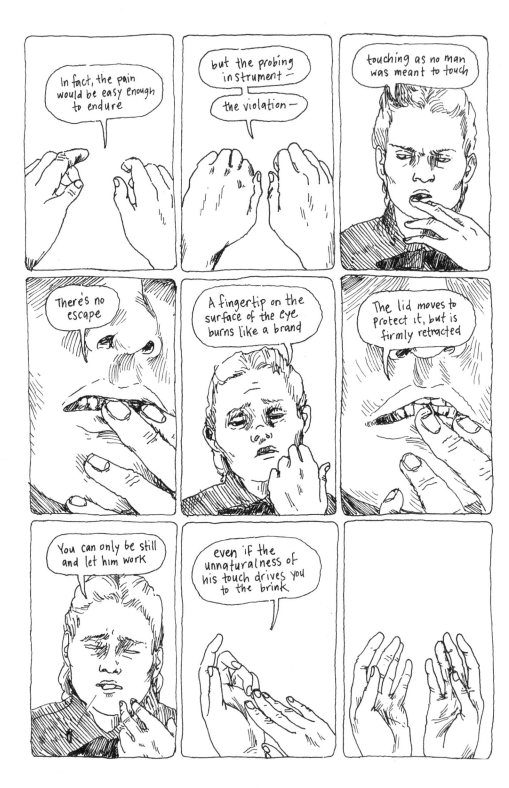

It felt like that.
How could you?
How could you let him touch you like that?
Like...?
It hurts —
KKrrr
You're hurting me —
Stop! Stop it!
KKKKrrr
KRKK

Miss
I'm off to the butcher's now, Miss.
The doctor stopped by to see Mrs. Lutz, but if he's done his visit before I'm back, then Beth will see him out.
That's fine.
Thanks, Matthew.
There's some extra in the food budget if you see a something nice
I trust your judgment.
Yes Miss

Hello. How's my patient?
Don't ask me, I've been down here doing the books.
I've seen Cora already — I was referring to yourself.
oh, hmm
I'm fine, A little sore.
May I take a look?
Of course.

It's healing excellently.
You'll be able to enjoy the sunshine again soon
Thank god! It's stuffy in this house.
It's stuffy in the city, too, I'm afraid.
But you grew up here, didn't you? You're used to the city.
Yes, Robert and I were raised here. But until last year I had planned to escape...
Harry's childhood home was by the sea... I suppose that will go to his sister now.
All those lost futures
How like dreams they fade.

What on Earth
my paper weight
It was on my desk

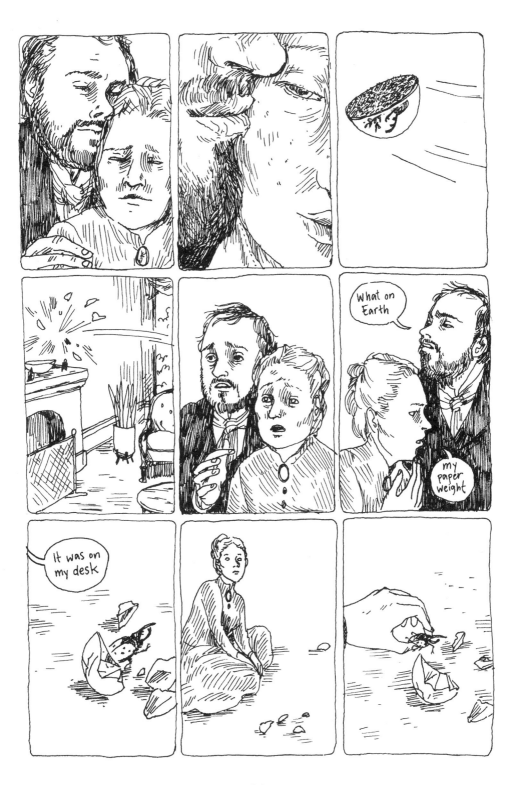

Something's different about you.
Me? I can't think what.
It's something, I can always tell. You're not ill?
Not at all. A little tired, I suppose.
That must be it.
That's what you get for staying up 'til all hours of the night and disturbing the rest of us.
It's bad enough for my health — maybe you don't realize how fragile I am —
or maybe you don't care —
but it's bad for your own health as well
You're much more likely to get sick when you don't sleep
If that matters to you.

I'm quite well and I sleep plenty but you're sweet to be concerned.
Of course I worry for you, Ella, much as I envy you your vigor.
Don't worry too much on my account
Fretful thoughts are the enemy of a strong constitution
You're very wise to say so.
Yes, I'm sure you can manage yourself.
Indeed you've always been a lucky one, blessed with wisdom as well as vitality
but you really must promise me that at the very first sign of illness you'll do whatever's necessary to get well at once.
To be sure.

In my fragile condition I can hardly risk being exposed to additional hardship
so threadbare is the seam that binds body to spirit
Even something so mean as a chill could tear it quite asunder
Indeed!
Well, to be on the safe side, a little hot wine before bed might be just the thing.
Not too hot.
You must stir it a little to let it cool before you serve it. Last time I nearly burned my tongue.
Last time you didn't even drink it! You screamed and spat it out!
So dramatic, Eleanor.
That's all the more reason to be more careful with it this time.

Here we are!
And your medicine's all mixed in!
No need to dribble it all over!
Why are there two?
This one's for me!
I'm going to drink it all up and have a nice long sleep, like you said!

Damn you! Where are you?
Don't you leave me here you bastard
huh huh huh huhh

uhh uhuhuhaaah
uhuhuaah
no no no
uhhhuhh
ahahaaa uhhh
nooo nooo ooo
Uhhhuhhuhoo
oooh ohh nooo

ahuh uh huh
ahuh
huhuhuuuoo
uhuh uh h h h
uhhhh
uhhhh
Robert?
what's wrong?
uhhh uhuhh uhuh

NOT LOST BUT
GONE BEFORE

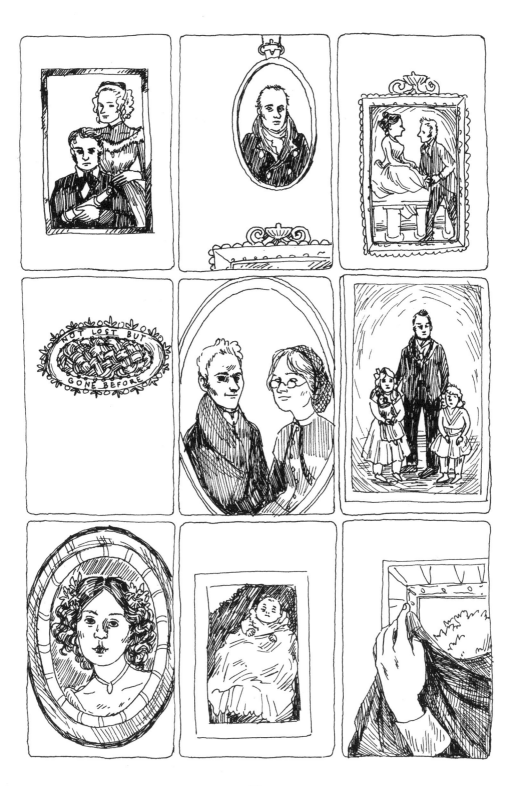

but I don't understand
shouldn't someone have been with her?
Actually, yes, the sister.
Eleanor?
Yes, but don't say anything
poor girl
I'm sure she blames herself

Please convey to your brother our deepest sympathies.
Both of your parents are gone as well, aren't they?
They are.
How sad. Your older brother must be a great comfort to you.
Younger, actually. But yes.
Still, the man is a pillar of strength in a home.
No doubt we'd be lost without each other.

Don't leave me, Ella
All my life
everyone always leaves me...
But not you. Isn't that right?
What are you saying?
Promise me
I promise
Did you hear something?
I'll go and look.

Beth, what happened?
I don't know, Miss.
The chairs, they...
they just up and moved.
Well, that seems very unlikely.
It happened too quick to really see.
I'm sorry it disturbed you, Miss.
It's all right, Beth. You can go to bed.
I'll sit up with her tonight.

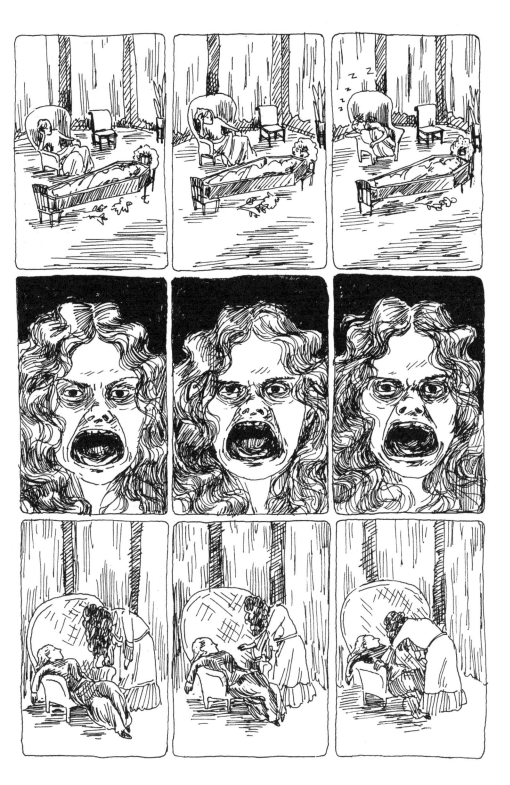

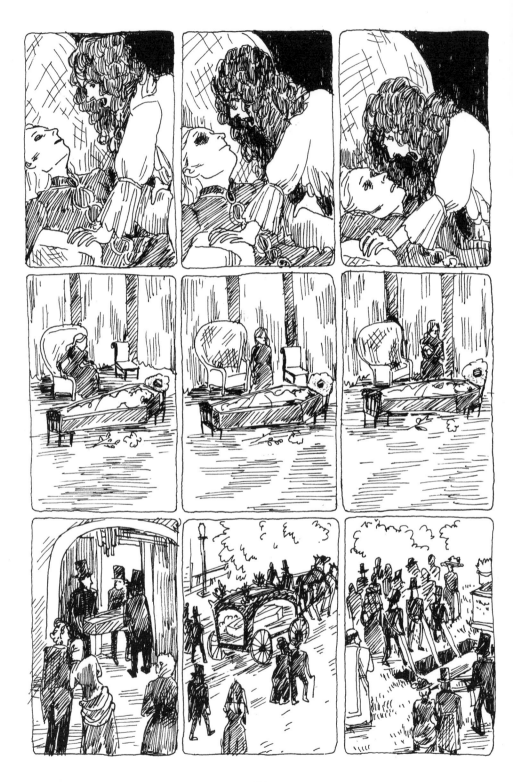

so the next time I see you will be to remove the cataract for good
I'll be very pleased to do it:
But Eleanor...
Please don't think me completely indecent...
Might I be permitted, at some time, to make a social call?
oh! Well, I — well, yes, of course.
we do know each other socially
I think I would like very much to know you better still.
Yes... I too...

I'm sorry, forgive me
no
don't stop
don't you dare

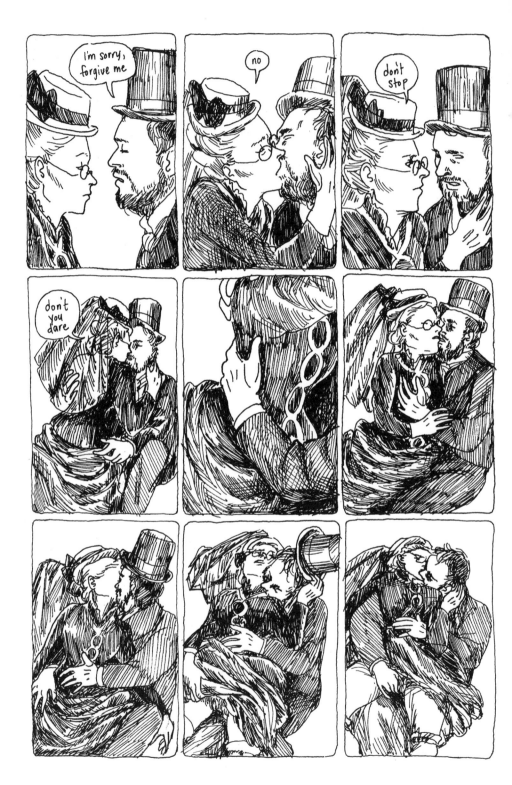

ah
ah
ahhh
ah, we're here,

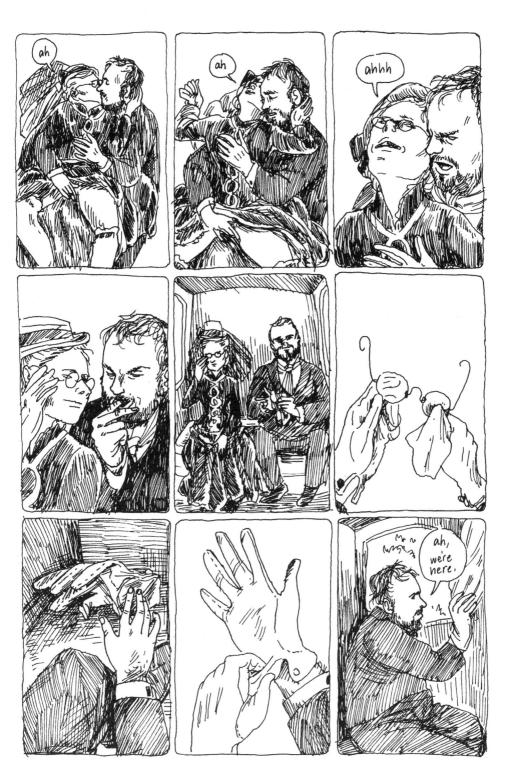

Thanks again for sharing the cab.

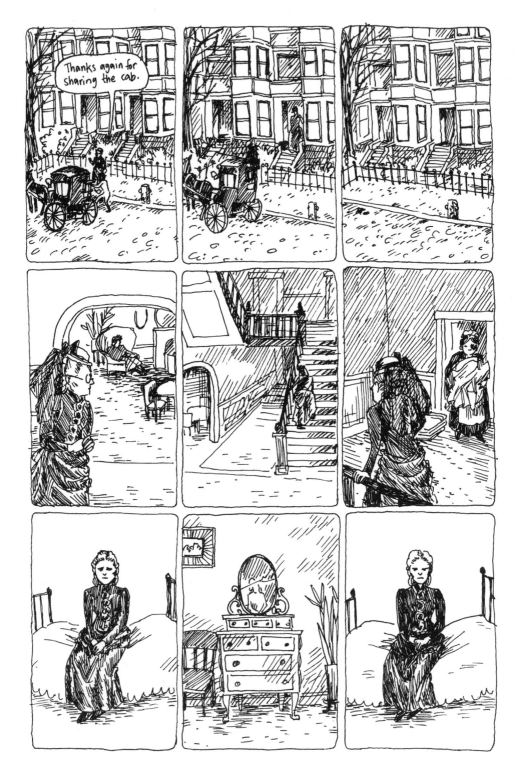

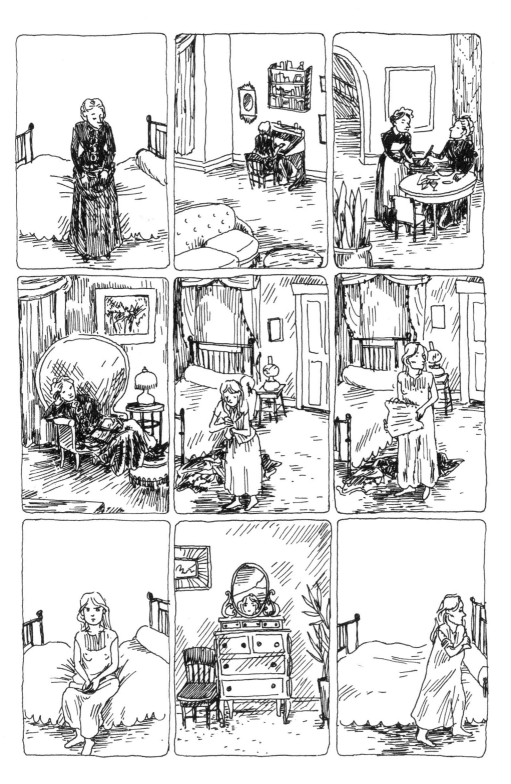

Z Z Z Z Z Z

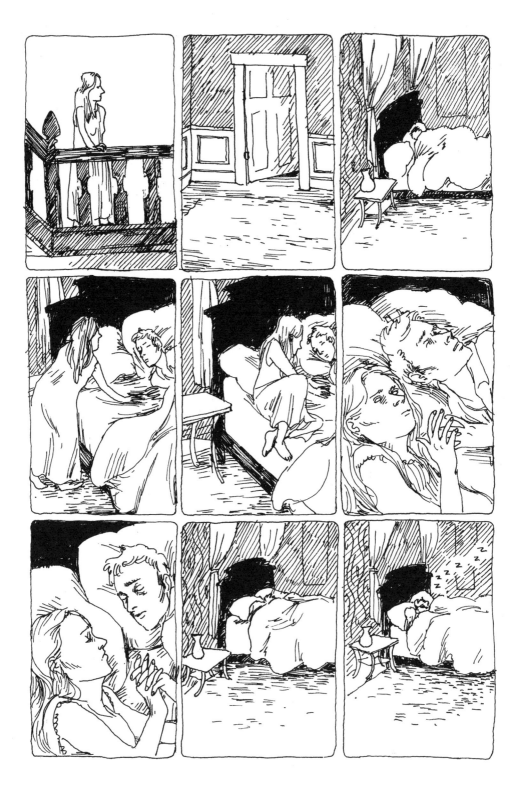

Robert!
what are you DOING!
stop it!
STOP
what?
You were...
I...
You were dreaming.
Go back to sleep.
I'm all wet from your spit.
Go to sleep

Mother died in this bed.
You mean Cora?
who?
Cora. Your wife.
No. Mother,
I saw her.
You were just a baby.
I saw her.
Every night in this bed I dream of her.
I brought you something to drink.

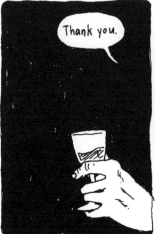

Thank you.

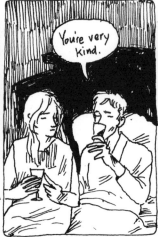

You're very kind.

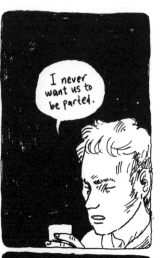

I never want us to be parted.

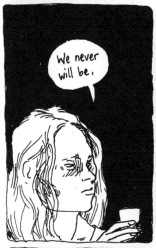

We never will be.

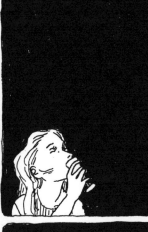

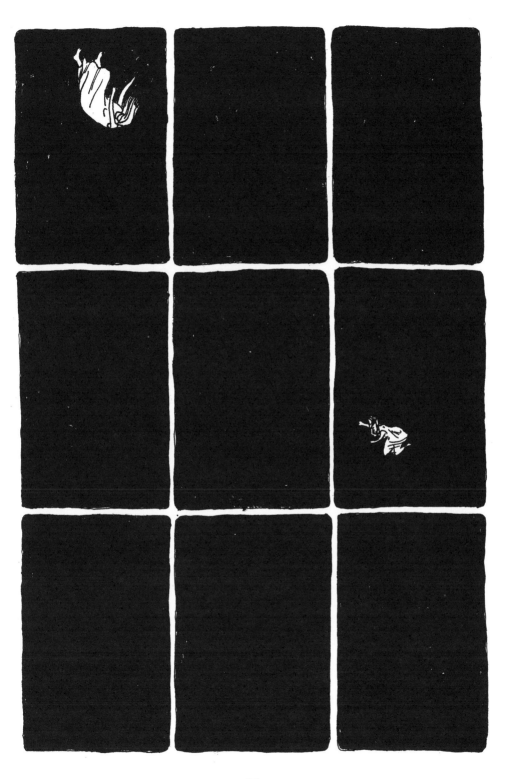

87

Julia Gfrörer ("grow fairer") is a writer and artist from New Hampshire. Her comics have appeared in *Cicada Magazine*, *Kramers Ergot*, and three volumes of *Best American Comics*. She self-publishes minicomics under the imprint Thuban Press, and her two other graphic novels, *Laid Waste* and *Black Is the Color*, are also available from Fantagraphics Books. She lives in New York with writer Sean T. Collins and their beautiful children.

With thanks to Pim, Frankenstein, Hellraiser, Gretchen, Hazel, and Sara.

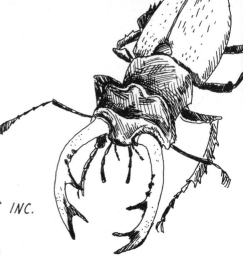

FANTAGRAPHICS BOOKS INC.
7563 Lake City Way NE
Seattle, Washington, 98115
www.fantagraphics.com

Editor and Associate Publisher: Eric Reynolds
Book Design: Justin Allan-Spencer
Production: Paul Baresh
Publisher: Gary Groth

ISBN 978-1-68396-315-8
Library of Congress Control Number 2019954477
First printing: September 2020
Printed in Hong Kong